Lionel
and the
Lion's Share

For R & R – *L.P.*

For my daughters, Neve and Isla – *L.S.*

First published 2018 by Nosy Crow Ltd, The Crow's Nest,
14 Baden Place, Crosby Row, London SE1 1YW
www.nosycrow.com

ISBN 978 1 78800 092 5 (HB)
ISBN 978 1 78800 093 2 (PB)

Nosy Crow and associated logos are trademarks and/or registered trademarks of Nosy Crow Ltd.

Text © Lou Peacock 2018
Illustrations © Lisa Sheehan 2018

The right of Lou Peacock to be identified as the author of this work
and of Lisa Sheehan as the illustrator of this work has been asserted.

A CIP catalogue record for this book is available from the British Library.

Printed in China by Imago

Papers used by Nosy Crow are made from wood grown in sustainable forests.

1 3 5 7 9 8 6 4 2 (HB)
1 3 5 7 9 8 6 4 2 (PB)

Lionel
and the
Lion's Share

LOU PEACOCK

ILLUSTRATED BY
LISA SHEEHAN

nosy crow

Lionel was a lion who did not
like to share.

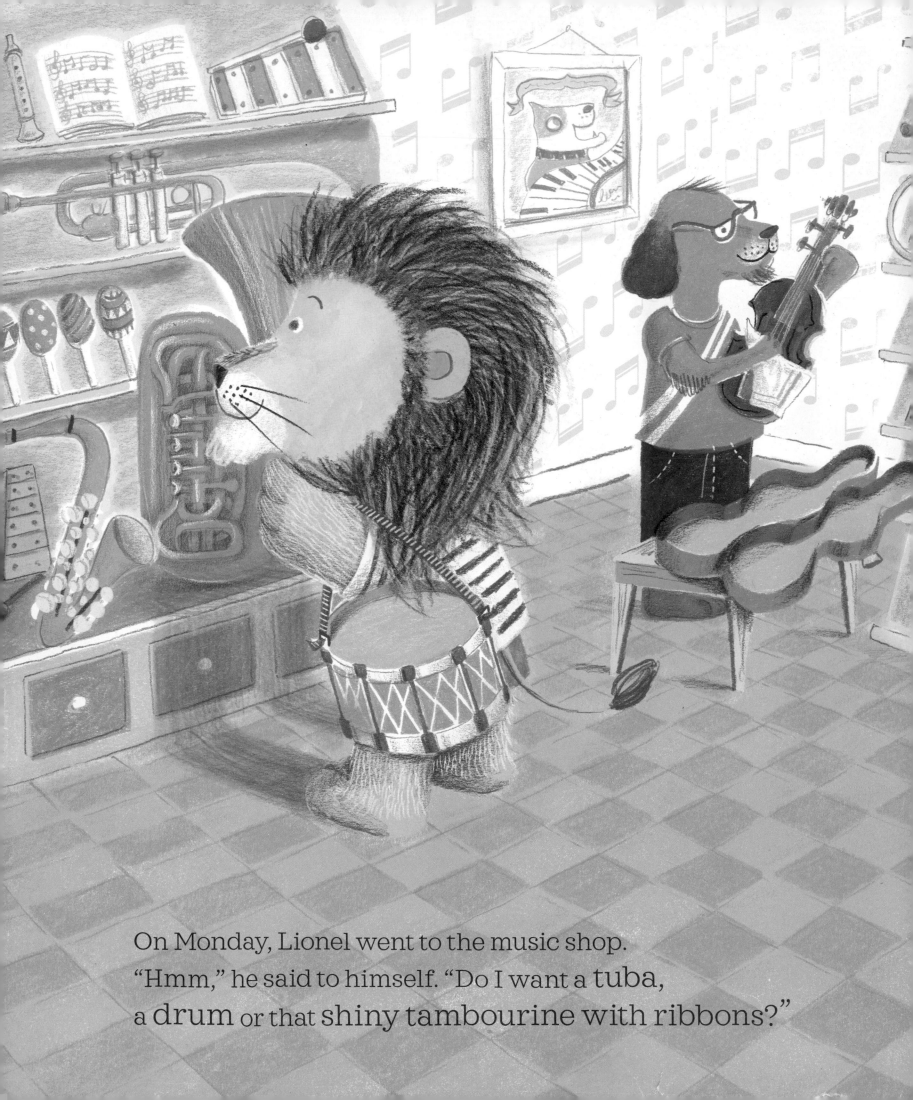

On Monday, Lionel went to the music shop.
"Hmm," he said to himself. "Do I want a tuba,
a drum or that shiny tambourine with ribbons?"

Elsa was in the shop, too, and she was just reaching out for the shiny tambourine with ribbons, when . . .

... Lionel snatched it.

"That's not fair, Lionel," said Elsa.

"You don't need a tuba, a drum **and** a tambourine.
You can't play those instruments all at once."

"But I am a **lion**," said Lionel.
"And I get the **lion's share.**
Anyway, I can play them all at once!"

And then he jingled and jangled
out of the shop.

"I **wish** Lionel would share," sighed Elsa.

On Tuesday, Lionel went to the hat shop.
He only needed one hat, but the hats were
SO beautiful that Lionel couldn't resist.

He bought four, five, six,
seven, eight, nine, ten hats.

Benji wanted a hat, too.
He had his eye on a
banana hat, when . . .

... Lionel snatched it.

"That's not fair, Lionel," said Benji.

"You only need one hat.
You can't wear all those hats at once."

"But I am a **lion**," said Lionel.
"And I get the **lion's share**.
Anyway, I can wear them all at once!"

And then he wibbled and wobbled out of the shop.

"I **wish** Lionel would share," sighed Benji.

On Wednesday, Lionel went
to the balloon stall. He thought
that the orange balloon was best,
but then he saw the red one.

And then he spotted the blue one and
the yellow one and the green one and
the purple one with silver stars.

Rosie was just reaching up for the
purple balloon with silver stars, but . . .

. . . Lionel was bigger,
and he got there first.

"That's not fair, Lionel," said Rosie.

"You don't need six balloons, and you
can't even hold them all at once."

"But I am a **lion**," said Lionel.
"And I get the **lion's share.**
Anyway, I **can** hold them all at once!"

And then he bobbed and
bounced all the way home.

"I **wish** Lionel would
share," sighed Rosie.

The next day was Thursday and Chloe was having
a birthday party with a **very big birthday cake.**

"I love cake!" said Lionel.
"And I am a **lion** so I get . . .

… the lion's share."

And he ate the **whole** cake!

But this time Lionel had gone too far.
And Chloe started to cry.

"Lionel," said Elsa, Rosie and Benji,
"we wish you would share.
And you won't."

"But I am a lion," said Lionel.

"We know," said Benji, "but that doesn't matter.
You took all the instruments and all the hats
and all the balloons, and now you've made Chloe cry.

You are a mean lion."

Lionel was furious.
And he stomped out of
the door.

But by the time he got home,
Lionel wasn't angry any more.

He was **sad**.

"I am a lion," said Lionel.
"And I have the lion's share . . .

but . . . I don't have any friends."

Suddenly, Lionel knew exactly what to do.
And off he went . . .

At Chloe's party, Chloe and Elsa and
Rosie and Benji were feeling sad, too.

When the door opened, and there was . . .

. . . Lionel.

He jingled and jangled, wibbled and wobbled,
and bobbed and bounced through the door.

"I am sorry," said Lionel. "You were right.
I was a mean lion, but look . . .

I've brought
all my instruments
and all my hats
and all my balloons . . .

...and they are for us **all** to share."

"Thank you, Lionel," said Chloe and Elsa and Rosie and Benji. "You are a very kind lion."

"Yes," 'ion . . ."

" . . . And lions **share!**"